Captain Jack
and the Pirates

For Theo, Tara, and Rosie — P.B.

For Anna Collette — H.O.

DIAL BOOKS FOR YOUNG READERS
Published by the Penguin Group
Penguin Group (USA) LLC
375 Hudson Street, New York, New York 10014

USA / Canada / UK / Ireland / Australia / New Zealand / India / South Africa / China
penguin.com
A Penguin Random House Company

First published in the United States 2016 by Dial Books for Young Readers
Originally published in Great Britain 2015 by Puffin Books
Text copyright © 2015 by Peter Bently
Pictures copyright © 2015 by Helen Oxenbury

CIP available upon request

Manufactured in China on acid-free paper
1 3 5 7 9 10 8 6 4 2

Captain Jack and the Pirates

PETER BENTLY & HELEN OXENBURY

Dial Books for Young Readers ⚲ an imprint of Penguin Group (USA) LLC

Jack, Zack, and Caspar,
brave mariners three,
were building a galleon down by the sea.

Up rose the sides
and the stern and the bow.
Zack, the ship's bosun, worked hard
on the prow.

A stick for the mainmast
and one for the yard . . .

Tying the two sticks together was hard.

A shirt
  and a bib,
    an inflatable ring . . .

For cannons, three buckets were
            just the right thing.

And there stood the galleon, fit for the fray,
as brave Captain Jack ordered,
"Anchors aweigh!"

They hoisted the mainsail,
    the flag was unfurled,
and Jack and his pirates set off round the world.

    Through oceans unknown,
        many miles from the land,
    sailed swashbuckling Jack and his buccaneer band.

"Ahoy, men!" cried Jack with a chortle of pleasure.
     "An enemy pirate ship,
          laden with treasure!"

"Steer a course after them, good Bosun Zack!"
     And Zack answered brightly,
          "Aye, aye, Captain Jack!"

"Caspar, take care of the cannons!" Jack said.
"Look sharp in the crow's nest, Cabin Boy Ted!"

As they closed in, every man did his duty,
hungry for glory and enemy booty.

Their proud pirate flag
        fluttered high in the breeze –
and then the ships sailed
        into stormier seas . . .

The wind became stronger.
        "Hold on to the sail!"
cried Jack as they battled a tropical gale.

Down came the rain
as the **hurricane** roared.
Down came the sail,
and then . . .

. . . man overboard!

The sides of the galleon started to slip.
"Quick!" cried the captain.
"Abandon the ship!"

Jack and his shipmates all struggled ashore.
"We're **marooned** on an island," he cried.
"Let's explore!"

"Those enemy pirates
were shipwrecked here too.
Let's hunt for their treasure!"
said Jack to his crew.

"Caspar, stay here while
we see what we find."
Said Zack, "Just in case
we're attacked from behind."

The captain and bosun spied out the view.
And then a loud voice cried out —

Jack,
is that you?

"The enemy pirates!"
hissed Jack to his mate.
"We must rescue Caspar
before it's too late!"

They ran down the hill
    and Jack cried, "Oho!
Brave little Caspar
    has seen off the foe!"

"And, look, here's their hideout!"
    Jack hollered with joy.
"The pirates have fled, lads,
            and . . ."

" . . . treasure ahoy!"

Jack and his shipmates
all gasped in delight
as they hungrily stared
at the glorious sight.

"Right, let's divide up our booty," said Jack.

"Caught you!" a voice cried.

The pirates

were

back!

There was no point
in struggling.

Their hopes were all wrecked.

Jack sighed,
"Now we'll all walk the plank,
I expect."

But those pirates were friendly.
They shared out their treasure—

and added **three** ice creams . . .

. . . just for good measure!